MW00947639

Meet
Mr. Eric M. Rogers, Author

Greetings,

My name is Eric Rogers, and it is with great pleasure that I introduce myself.

I would like to share my experience in the field of Early Childhood Education. My journey in early childhood began when I received my Bachelor's Degree in Interdisciplinary Studies: ECE/Math from Norfolk State University in 1996. My professional experience was then further enriched as I have taught and been a Center Director in Virginia, New York and Georgia. Through my leadership, I have supported several Early Childhood Education Learning Centers in receiving National Accreditation which helped build and cultivate quality experiences for children, teachers and families. As such, I am very proud of those accomplishments, just as I am with finally completing my first children's book "IN MY HOUSE" and now "EVA & WILLIE"

Overall, I have over 25 years of experience in the education field (20 years as a Center Director and the other years as a Preschool teacher and Afterschool Director for multiple locations).

My goals have always been to ensure every child feels secure, included and respected as they go through their early childhood experiences. "Eva & Willie" is another tool that will be available to help teach manners, confidence, and build selfesteem. Children deserve to have fun while learning in an environment where they feel safe and respected.

So I hope this book brings as much pleasure for you and your family, as it was for me to produce one of my dreams for you.

Respectfully,

Eric M. Rogers

Whole Child. Passionate Teachers. Confident Parent.

About This Book

Eva & Willie is a tool for teaching social-emotional development such as empathy, confidence, self-esteem (loving yourself), and gratitude.

Eva & Willie are best friends that meet at "the bench" in the park every weekend to take a walk and talk about what's happening in their lives. During their walk, they come upon "Grasshopper," "Swan," "The twin cats," "Butterfly," "Pony," and "Fish." Willie (the parrot) teaches Eva (the dog) how to use good manners (speaking to others when passing them, saying "thank you" when someone does kind gestures and "excuse me" when you accidently bump into someone or walk directly in front or behind them).

Eva and Willie © 2020 Eric Rogers. All rights reserved.
No part of this publication may be reproduced, stored in a retrieval system, or transmitted, in any form, or by any means, electronic, mechanical, photocopying, recording, or otherwise, without the prior consent of the author.

My book, *Eva & Willie*, is dedicated
to the life, love, and memories I received
from my Mother & Grandmother

Ethel Mae "Eva"
Heart Rogers
– Mother of the Author

Willie Mae "Willie" Heart –
Grandmother of the Author

My mother was a huge part of helping me build confidence and self-esteem. She also taught me the importance of manners. She would always tell me how her mother taught her these life lessons as well.

"Charlie, Joedy, Margary & Tamiko,

Sure as you come, you must go and if I go first, please don't cry and get yourself sick. I have done my job so far and I am passing over to rest and that doesn't mean I am dead, because if all or one of you let me, I can live in you. I know because my mother lives in me.

Love your mother,
Eva Ethel M. Heart Rogers

P.S. Reach for the World!"

Song dedication to my mom:
"Never Would've Made It" by Marvin Sapp

Hi! My name is Eva, but Ianna calls me Lo-Lo. They're taking me to the park today. I'm excited to see my best friend Willie for our weekly walk in the park!

Hi there!! My name is Willie. Today is one of my favorite days. I'm meeting my best friend Eva. We are taking a walk and going to our favorite place to talk: "the bench." I wonder who we will see. I hope you enjoy our journey!

"Good morning, Grasshopper!" says Willie.
"Hi Willie! How are you?" says Grasshopper.
Eva continues to walk and does not speak.

Willie says, "Eva, why didn't you speak to Grasshopper? It's polite to speak to someone when you walk past them."

Eva says, "But I don't know Grasshopper."

Willie says, "Whether you know someone or not, it is always polite to speak when you pass someone."

Eva and Willie continue on their walk, and they come upon Swan. Swan says, "Hi Eva and Willie."

Eva and Willie both speak back. "Hi Swan!"

Eva tells Willie, "I wish I was as pretty as Swan. She's beautiful."

Eva and Willie continue their walk and come upon "The Twin Cats." The Cats, Eva, and Willie all speak to each other.

Eva tells Willie, "Look at their collars! They are amazing! I wish I had a collar like theirs."

Eva and Willie continue their walk and they come upon Butterfly. Butterfly lands on the flower to eat nectar. Nectar is food for butterflies.

Eva says, "WOW! Look at her wings. They are so beautiful. I wish I had wings like that."

They continue their walk and start getting closer and closer to the bench.

Eva is so excited to see the bench up ahead because she is ready to talk to her best friend about what's going on in her life. She accidently bumps into Pony, and Willie falls off her back. Eva continues to run towards the bench with excitement.

Willie says, "Eva, please slow down. We don't have to rush. We need to go back because you need to say excuse me or sorry to Pony."

"Why do we have to go back?" says Eva. "That was an accident."

"I know," says Willie. "That's why we have to go back. It's polite to say sorry and excuse me when you accidentally bump into someone."

So, Eva and Willie go back to apologize to Pony. "Sorry, Pony," says Eva.

"It's okay, Eva," says Pony, "but thank you for coming back and apologizing. That was very kind of you."

Eva and Willie continue walking towards the bench.

Right before Eva and Willie reach the bench, they come upon Fish. "Good afternoon, Fish," say Eva and Willie.

"It's nice to see you again. Eva, I like your collar," says Fish. Eva's collar has her name on it.

Eva is still excited to get to the bench. She just continues to walk towards the bench. Willie stops Eva and says, "You have to tell Fish 'Thank you.' He gave you a compliment. It's polite to say thank you when someone gives you something, does something nice for you, or gives you a compliment."

Eva tells Fish thank you and Fish says, "You're welcome."

Eva continues to the bench, excited to talk to her best friend.

Willie sits on the bench.

"What are you so excited to talk about today, Eva?" says Willie.

"Nothing," says Eva. "I'm always excited to talk to you. You are my best friend. I like talking to you."

"Come over to the pond," says Willie.

Eva and Willie walk over to the pond. Willie says to Eva, "During our walk I heard you say you wish you were as pretty as Swan, that the twins' collars were better than yours, and you wish you had wings like the butterfly. Look at yourself. There are things that are so amazing about you. Look at your eyes. Look at your ears. Look at your nose. You are beautiful. Admire things about yourself. Your differences and uniqueness, that's what makes you, you."

What do you like about yourself?

Activities

- Discussions: Children say something nice about a classmate. Other child says "Thank you."

- Act out manners (children saying thank you when someone does something for them, children saying excuse me when someone walk in front/behind someone. Children saying excuse me when they accidentally bump into someone else.)

- Children give Grasshopper, Swan, Cats, Butterfly, Pony, and Fish names.

- 2 Coloring pages included. Coloring book bought separately.

- Give children a mirror to pass around. Each child tells you what they like about themselves.

- Building Confidence: "Show & Tell" every Friday. Children must stand in front of his/her classmates and "show & tell" about the item they're presenting. Always have a microphone or a prop for a microphone.

- Good for Theme: All About Me

CPSIA information can be obtained at www.ICGtesting.com
Printed in the USA
BVIW121658070720
583140BV00020B/433